A P.U.R.S.T. ADVENTURE

KIDS CAN PRESS

FOR THE FABULOUS BAKER GIRLS: JULIA, MALIA AND IVORY.

Kids Can Press gratefully acknowledges the financial support of the Government of Ontario, through the Ontario Media Development Corporation; the Ontario Arts Council; the Canada Council for the Arts; and the Government of Canada, through the CBF, for our publishing activity.

Published in Canada and the U.S. by Kids Can Press Ltd.
25 Dockside Drive, Toronto, ON M5A 0B5

Kids Can Press is a Corus Entertainment Inc. company

www.kidscanpress.com

The artwork in this book was rendered digitally in between frequent walks and rounds of BALL!
The text is set in Fontoon.

Edited by Yasemin Uçar
Designed by Julia Naimska

Printed and bound in Shenzhen, China, in 10/2017 by C&C Offset

CM 18 0 9 8 7 6 5 4 3 2 1
CM PA 18 0 9 8 7 6 5 4 3 2 1

Library and Archives Canada Cataloguing in Publication

Spires, Ashley, 1978–, author, illustrator

Gordon : bark to the future! / written and illustrated by Ashley Spires. (A P.U.R.S.T. adventure)

ISBN 978-1-77138-409-4 (hardcover).--ISBN 978-1-77138-410-0 (softcover)

1. Graphic novels. I. Title. II. Series: Spires, Ashley, 1978– . P.U.R.S.T. adventure.

PN6733.S66G67 2018 j741.5'971 C2017-902756-5

NO WORMHOLES
OR TIME VORTEXES
WERE CREATED DURING
THE MAKING OF
THIS BOOK.

GORDON
BARK TO THE FUTURE!
by ASHLEY SPIRES

IT'S ALL UP TO GORDON NOW.

GORDON IDENTITY CONFIRMED
WOOOSH
LAB SECURED
BZZZZZZZZZZT
huffa huff
HIS PARTNER HAS BEEN CAPTURED.
MEORRR!
BZZZZZ

HIS SUPERIOR OFFICER HAS BEEN NEUTRALIZED.

AND GORDON'S DISTRESS CALLS TO P.U.R.S.T. (PETS OF THE UNIVERSE READY FOR SPACE TRAVEL) COMMAND CENTER ...

HAVE GONE UNANSWERED.

THEY DIDN'T SEE IT COMING.

THE ALIENS HATCHED IN THE WALLS.

THEY EMERGED IN THE NIGHT.

AND HIS HUMANS ...
BUZZ
AHHHHH!
HIS POOR HELPLESS HUMANS!
THEY GOT THERE AS FAST AS THEY COULD ...
BZZZZZ
ARGH! AHHHHH!
BUT IT WAS TOO LATE.

NOW HE IS A LONE SPACE PET ...

IN THE MIDDLE OF AN ALIEN INVASION.

PHYSICAL COMBAT HAS NEVER BEEN GORDON'S STRENGTH.

BETTER TO LEAVE THE LEAPING AND POUNCING TO THE CATS.

THIS DOG'S DEADLIEST WEAPON IS HIS MIND.

BUT NONE OF HIS COMPUTERS, ROBOTS OR DEVICES
COULD HAVE PREPARED HIM FOR THIS.

THINK, GORDON, THINK!

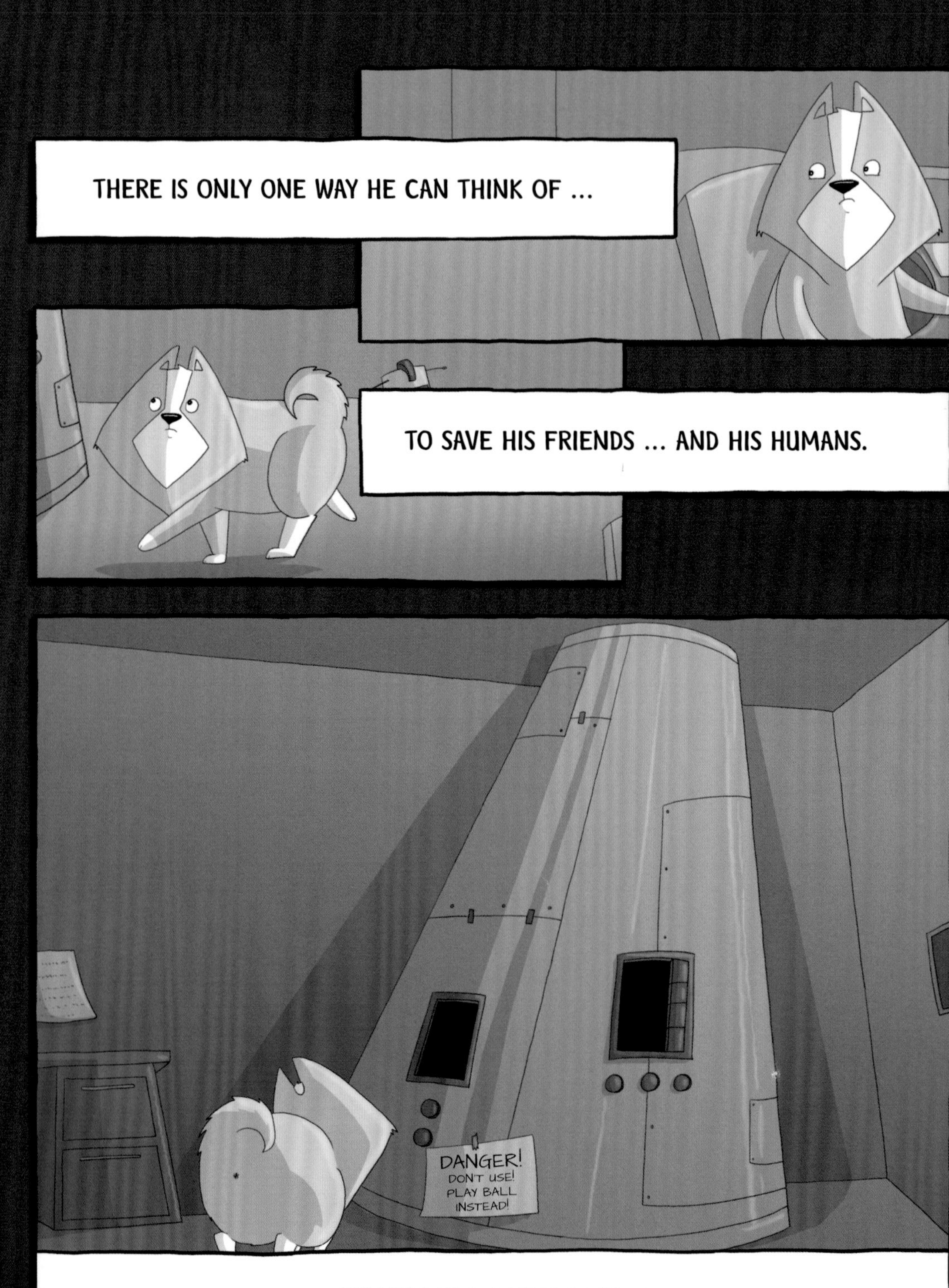
THERE IS ONLY ONE WAY HE CAN THINK OF ...
TO SAVE HIS FRIENDS ... AND HIS HUMANS.
DANGER!
DON'T USE!
PLAY BALL
INSTEAD!
BUT IT'S TOO DANGEROUS.

THE DEVICE ISN'T READY.
KROOSH
IT'S JUST A PROTOTYPE.
IT HASN'T EVEN BEEN TESTED!
AROOF.
DANGER! DON'T USE! PLAY BALL INSTEAD!
IF ONLY HE HADN'T SPENT SO MUCH TIME PLAYING BALL!

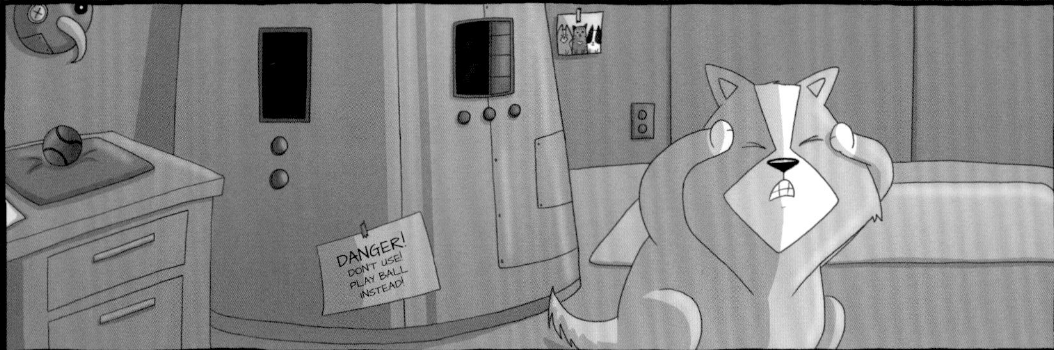

NOT NOW, GORDON! FOCUS!

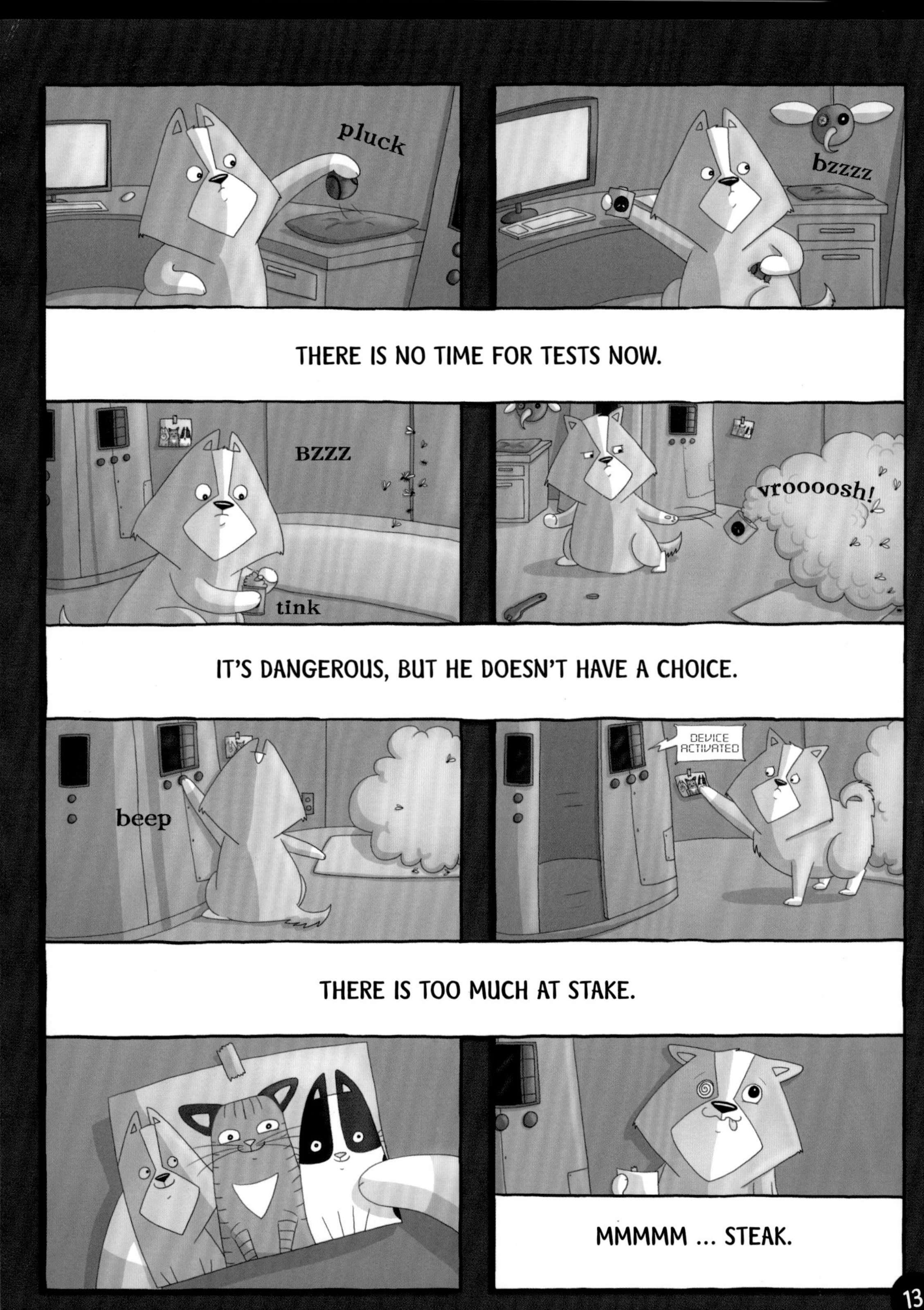
pluck
bzzzz
THERE IS NO TIME FOR TESTS NOW.
BZZZ
tink
vroooosh!
IT'S DANGEROUS, BUT HE DOESN'T HAVE A CHOICE.
beep
DEVICE ACTIVATED
THERE IS TOO MUCH AT STAKE.
MMMMM ... STEAK.

FOCUS!

THE ENEMY IS UPON HIM!

DOGGONE IT, HE NEEDS MORE TIME!

beep

AND THAT'S EXACTLY WHAT
HE'S GOING TO GET.

zoom
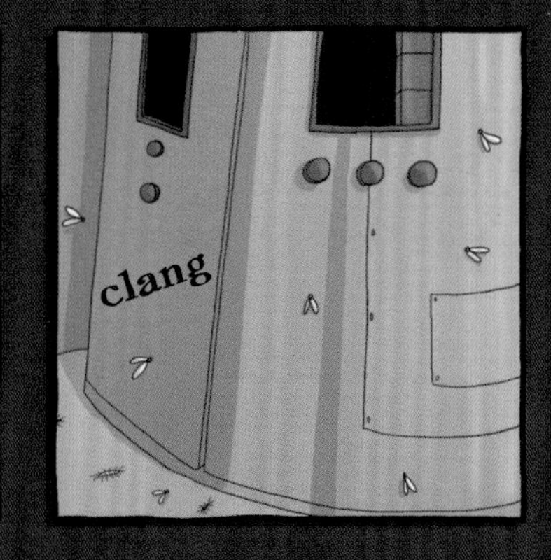
clang

TRAVEL BACK:
5 YEARS

WHIRR
click
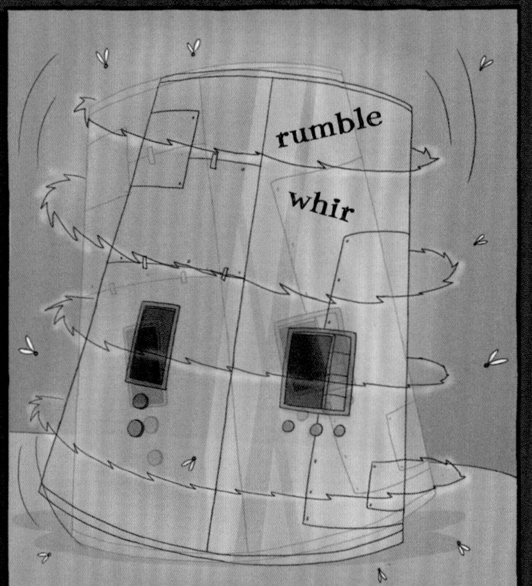
rumble
whir

SHAPOW!

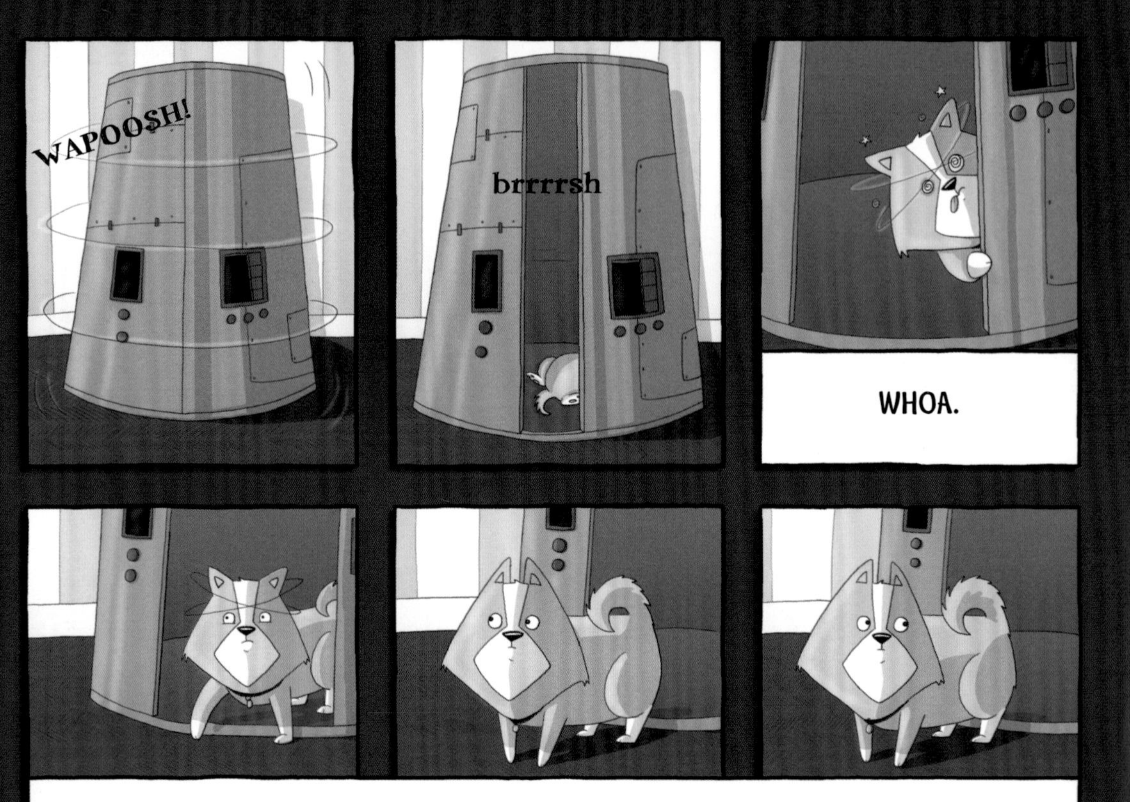
WAPOOSH!
brrrrsh
WHOA.
HE'S IN HIS SPACE STATION ... BUT THERE ARE NO ALIENS!

THIS CAN ONLY MEAN ONE THING ...
AROO!
GORDON'S TIME MACHINE WORKED!

NOW HE JUST NEEDS TO STOP THE ALIEN INVASION BEFORE IT STARTS.

BUT HE MUST BE CAREFUL NOT TO CHANGE ANYTHING ELSE.

IF HE CHANGES THE PAST TOO MUCH, HE COULD JEOPARDIZE THE FUTURE, WHICH IS, TECHNICALLY, HIS PRESENT BECAUSE HE'S IN THE PAST.

HOLY HAIR BALLS, THAT'S CONFUSING.

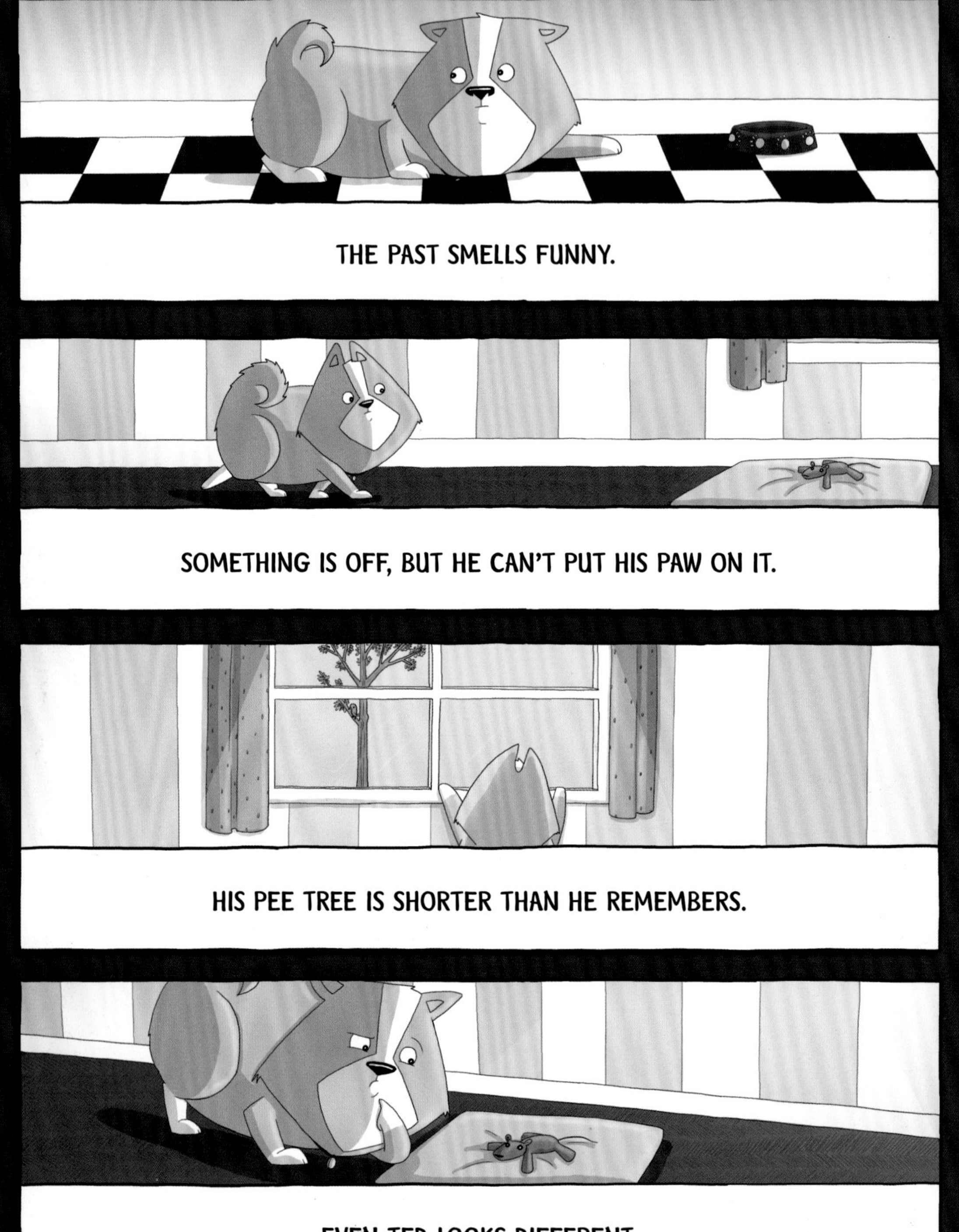
THE PAST SMELLS FUNNY.
SOMETHING IS OFF, BUT HE CAN'T PUT HIS PAW ON IT.
HIS PEE TREE IS SHORTER THAN HE REMEMBERS.
EVEN TED LOOKS DIFFERENT.

IT'S WEIRDLY QUIET, TOO.

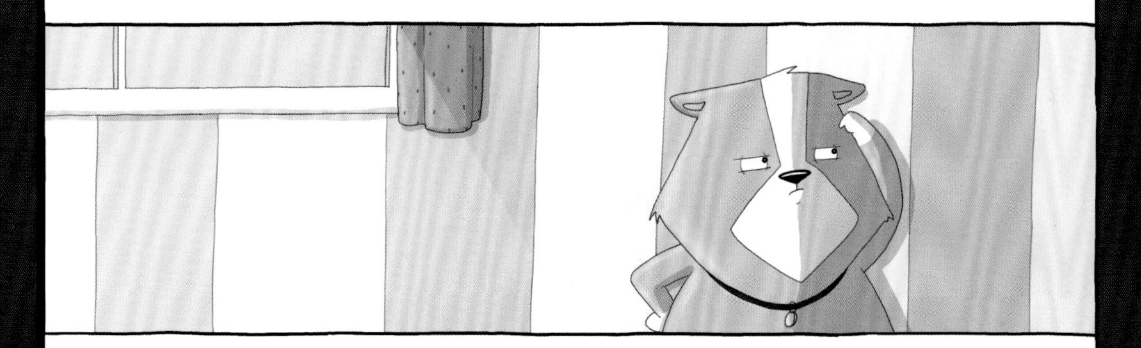

ALMOST LIKE SOMETHING IS MISSING ...

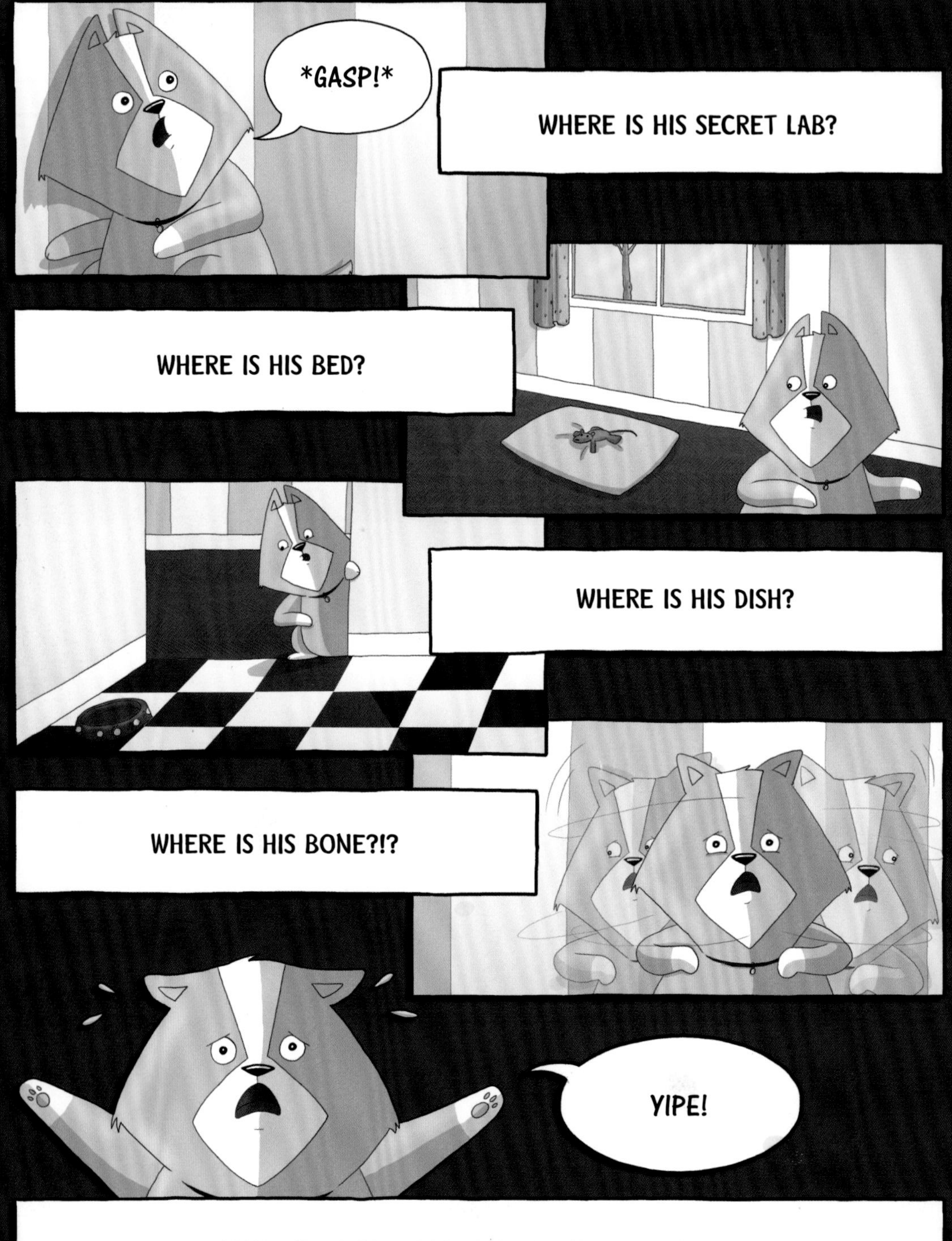
GASP!
WHERE IS HIS SECRET LAB?
WHERE IS HIS BED?
WHERE IS HIS DISH?
WHERE IS HIS BONE?!?
YIPE!
HOLY FUZZBUTT! GORDON DOESN'T LIVE HERE!

HOW COULD THIS HAVE HAPPENED?

HE WENT BACK TOO FAR!

FIVE YEARS TOO FAR!

FIVE YEARS AGO HE WASN'T EVEN BORN YET ...

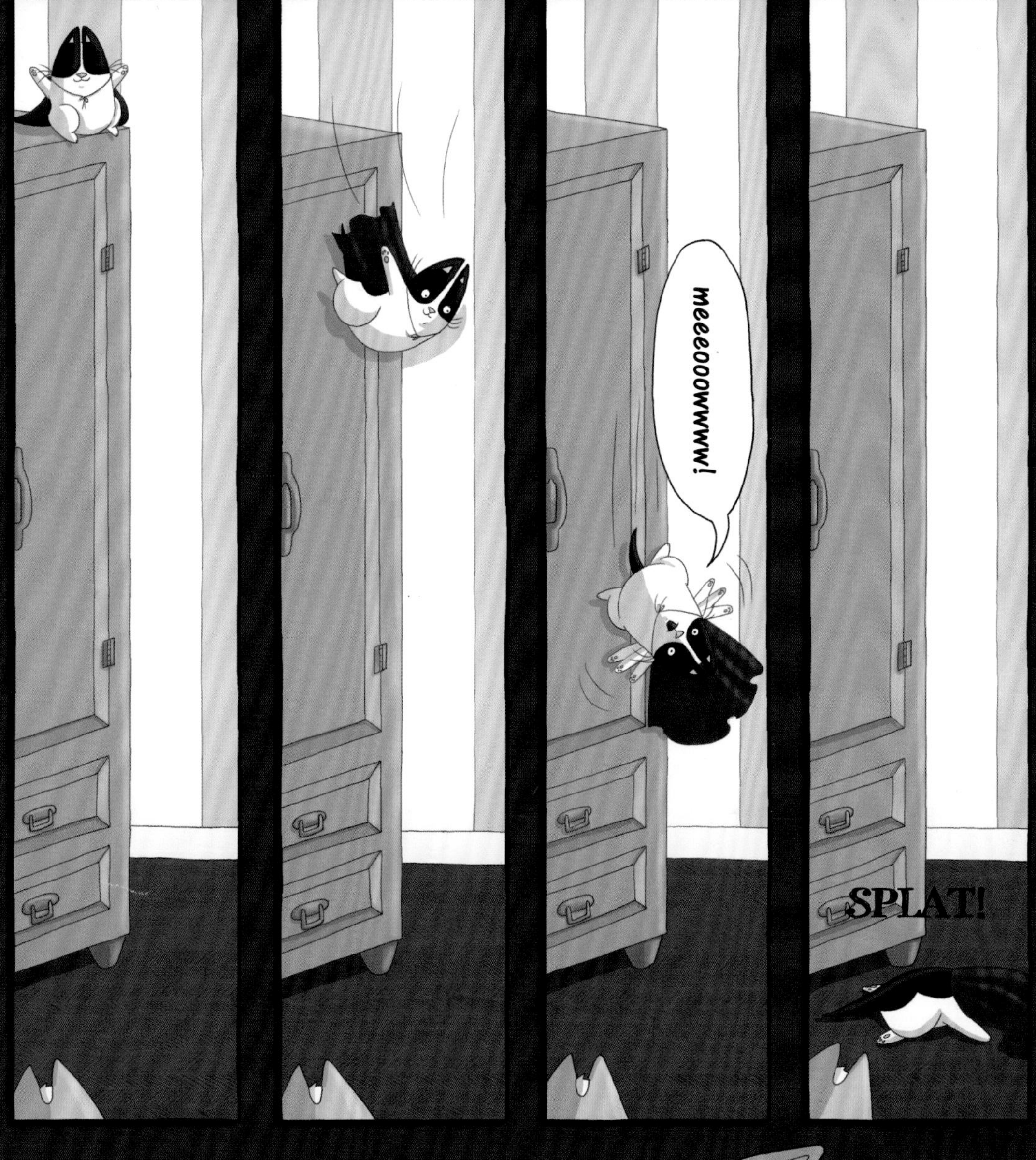

SOMETHING TELLS HIM THAT
BINKY WON'T BE MUCH HELP.

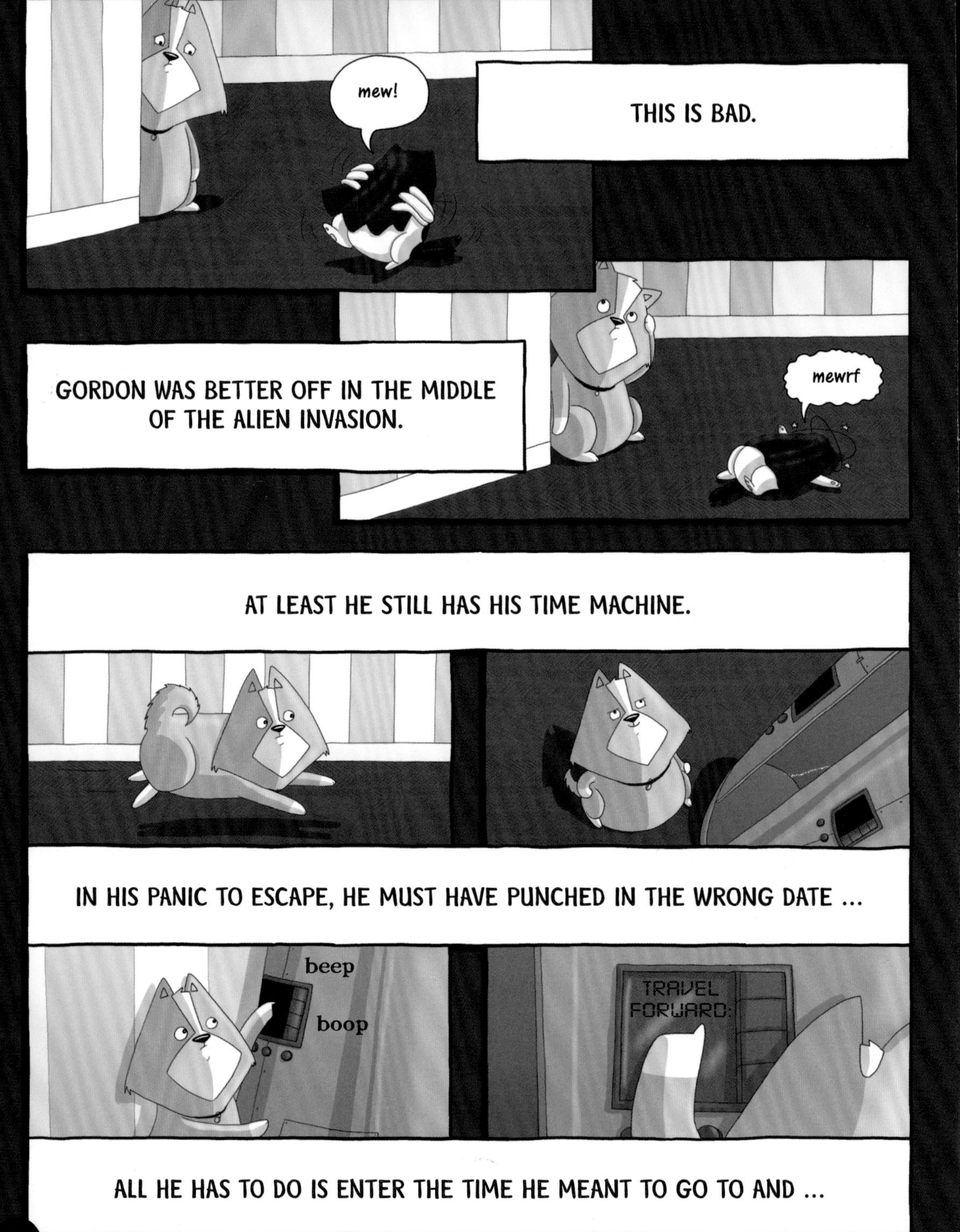
mew!
THIS IS BAD.
GORDON WAS BETTER OFF IN THE MIDDLE OF THE ALIEN INVASION.
mewrf
AT LEAST HE STILL HAS HIS TIME MACHINE.
IN HIS PANIC TO ESCAPE, HE MUST HAVE PUNCHED IN THE WRONG DATE ...
beep
boop
TRAVEL FORWARD:
ALL HE HAS TO DO IS ENTER THE TIME HE MEANT TO GO TO AND ...

UH-OH. THAT CAN'T BE GOOD.

NO POWER!

HE IS OUT OF ALLOFUZZIUM!*

*ALLOFUZZIUM IS A SUPER RARE TYPE OF FUEL.
ITS ONLY PURPOSE IS TO MAKE TIME MACHINES WORK.

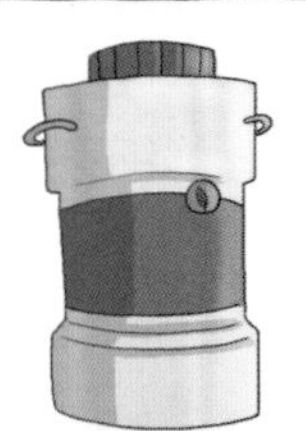

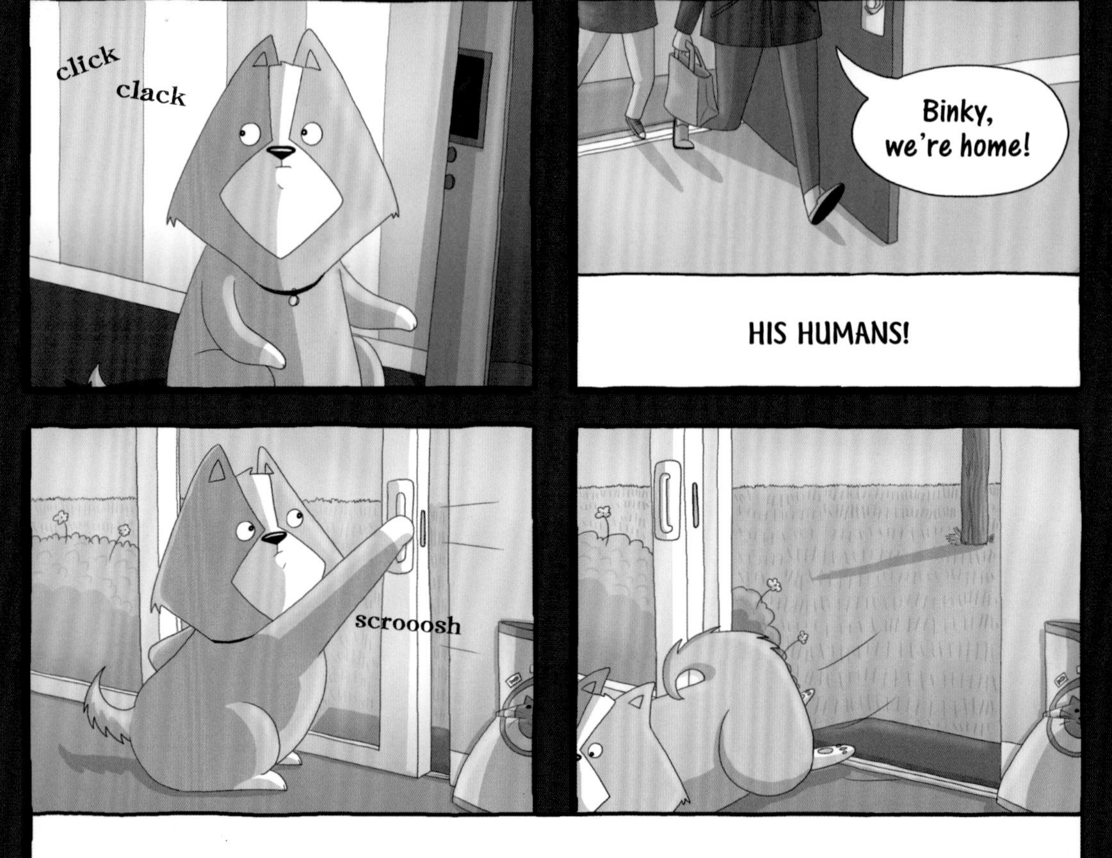
click
clack
Binky, we're home!
HIS HUMANS!
scroooosh
HE CAN'T LET THEM SEE HIM. THEY WON'T KNOW WHO HE IS!

ugh
nurgh
scrape
THEY MIGHT THINK HE'S LOST AND CALL ANIMAL CONTROL.

THUD
scrape
scrush
scroosh
Did you hear something?
There's nothing out there.
phew

HE HAS TO TRY TO CONTACT P.U.R.S.T. HEADQUARTERS.

SERGEANT FLUFFY VANDERMERE WILL KNOW WHAT TO DO.

THAT WAS WEIRD.

HOLY FUTURE FURBALLS! OF COURSE!

P. U.R.S.T. ISN'T P. U.R.S.T.!

IT'S STILL **F. U.R.S.T.** *FELINES* OF THE UNIVERSE READY FOR SPACE TRAVEL!

THEY HAVEN'T STARTED THEIR EQUAL OPPORTUNITY PROGRAM YET, WHICH MEANS ...

NO DOGS ALLOWED IN F.U.R.S.T. ...
OR HIS SPACE STATION.
I love you, Binky.
muurm
THE PAST NEEDS A POOP SCOOP BECAUSE THIS PLACE STINKS.

HE NEEDS TO REGROUP AND FIGURE A WAY OUT OF THIS.

HE WON'T BE GOING ANYWHERE UNLESS HE GETS SOME MORE ALLOFUZZIUM.

BUT HOW CAN HE FIND SOME WITHOUT P.U.R.S.T. ...

OR HIS LAB ...

OR HIS BONE ...

mmuuurrr

OR HIS FRIENDS?

WAIT A MINUTE ...
BINKY MIGHT JUST BE A KITTEN AND P. U.R.S.T. MIGHT NOT EXIST ...

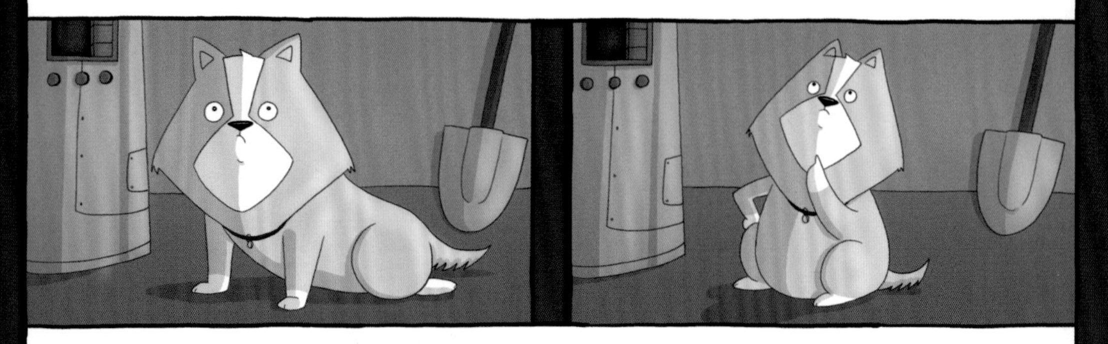

BUT CAPTAIN GRACIE IS OUT THERE SOMEWHERE.

GRACIE WILL HELP HIM. HE JUST KNOWS SHE WILL.

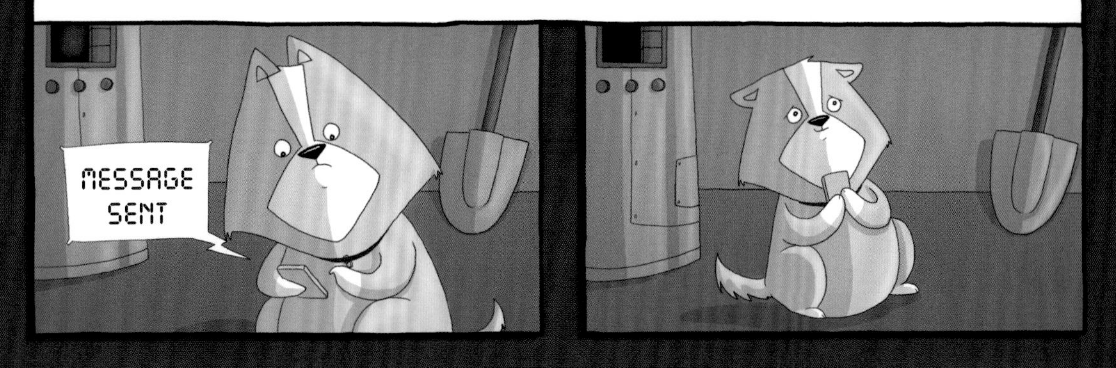

ALL HE HAS TO DO IS WAIT.

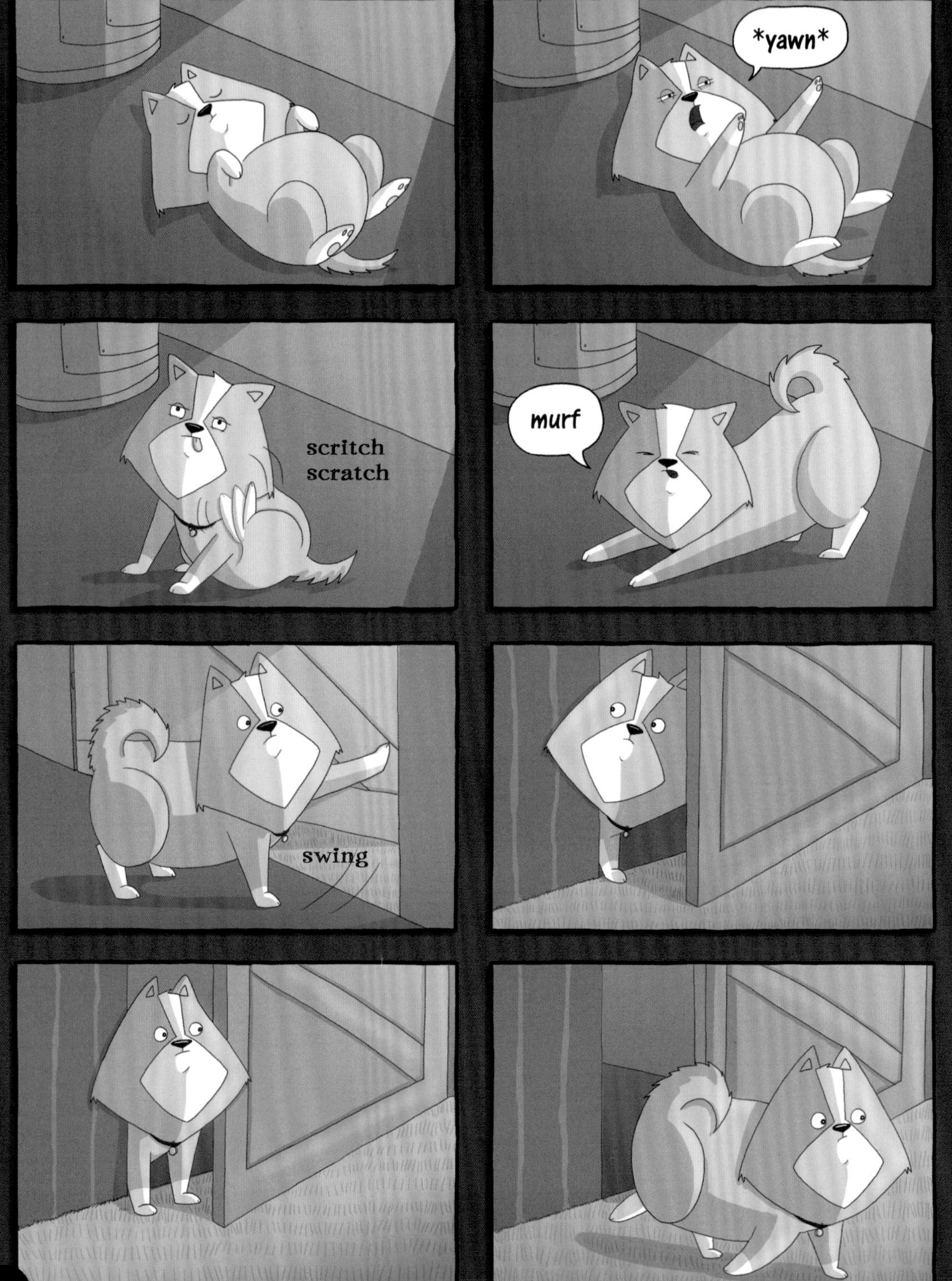
yawn
scritch
scratch
murf
swing

ploop
scrutch
IT'S A NEW DAY AND THIS DOG NEEDS A PLAN.

psssssss ...
HE MIGHT NOT LIVE HERE YET ...

sniff
sniff
pssssss ...
BUT THIS IS STILL HIS SPACE STATION.

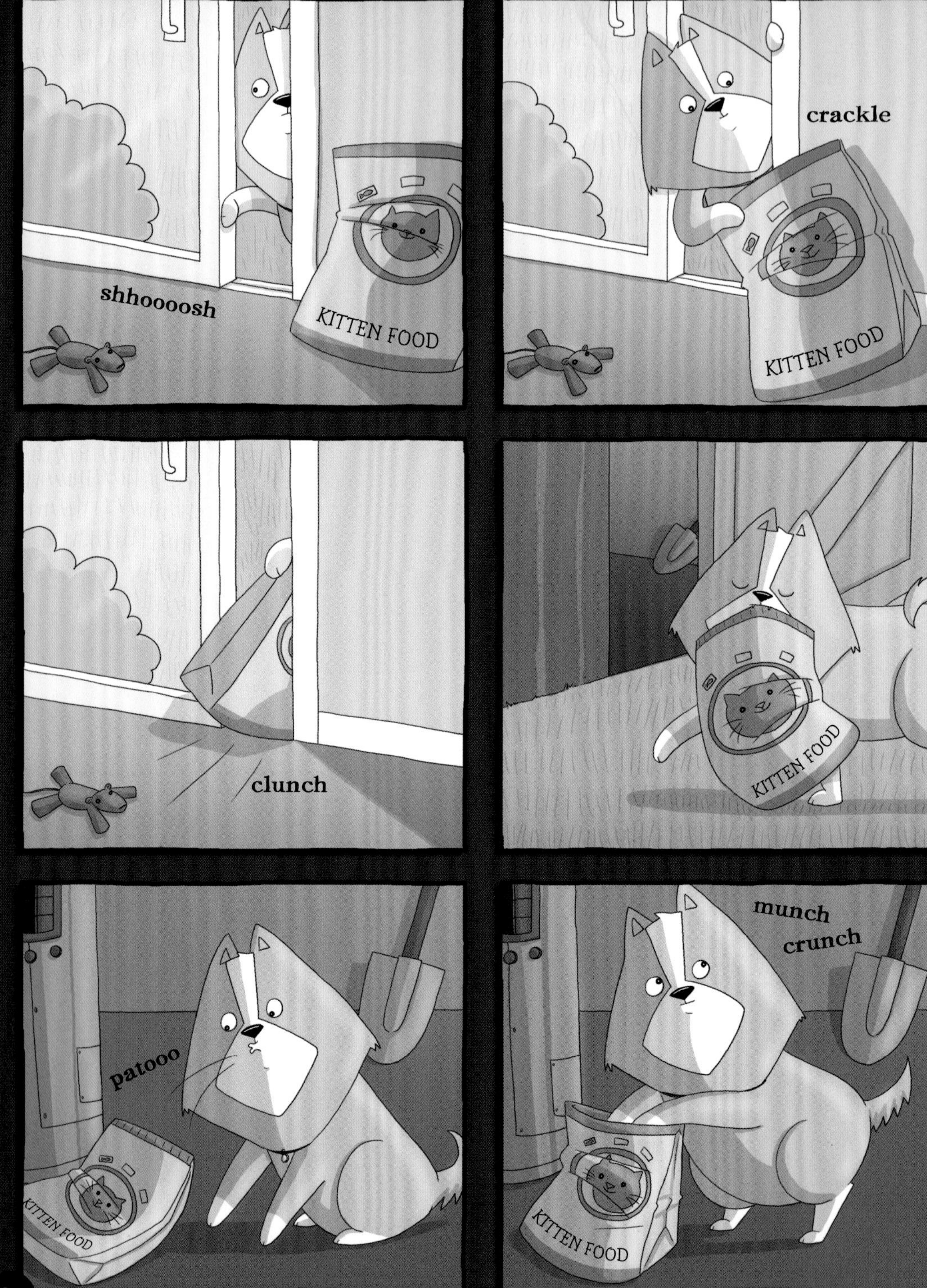
shhoooosh
KITTEN FOOD
crackle
KITTEN FOOD
clunch
KITTEN FOOD
patooo
KITTEN FOOD
munch
crunch
KITTEN FOOD

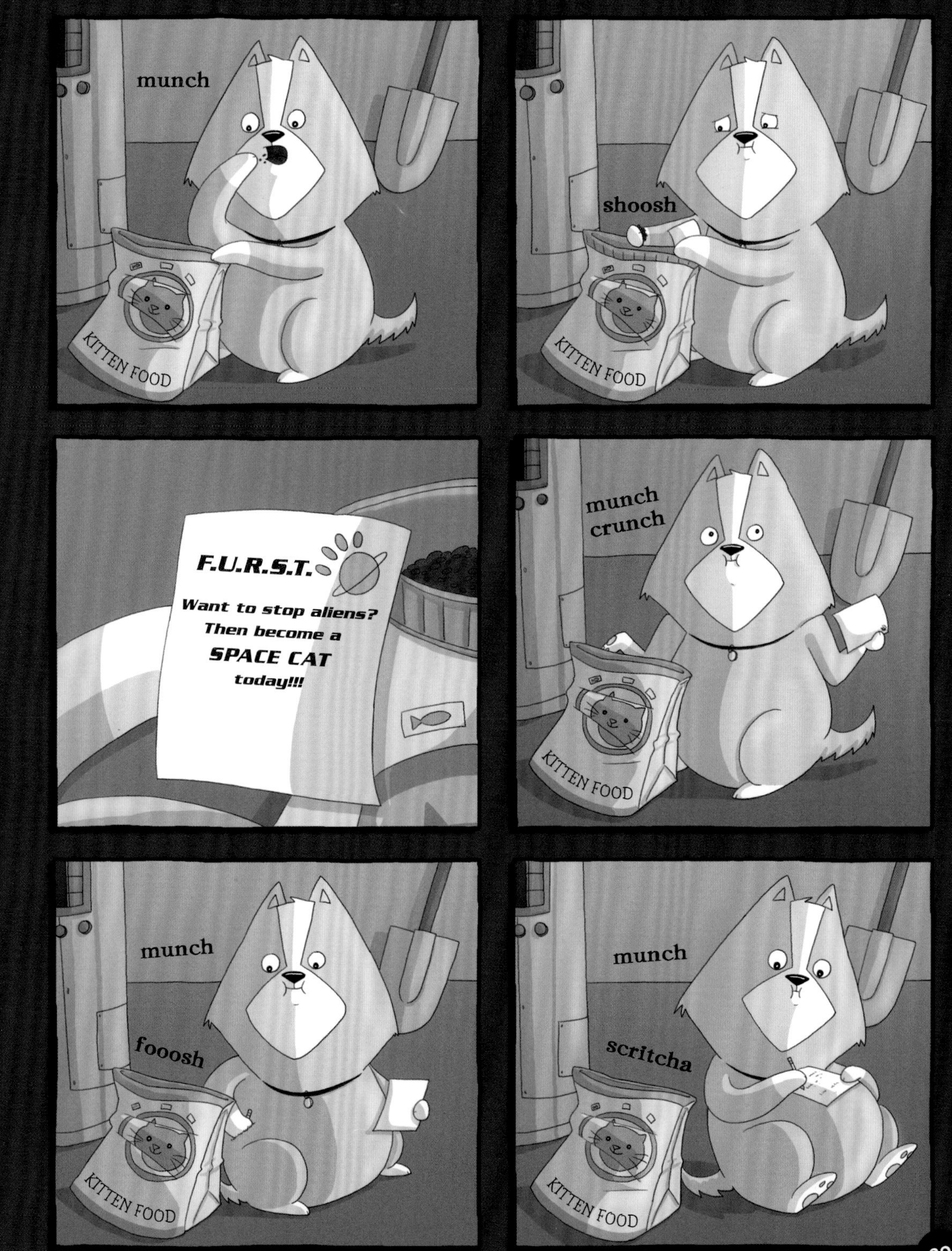
munch
KITTEN FOOD
shoosh
KITTEN FOOD
F.U.R.S.T.
Want to stop aliens?
Then become a
SPACE CAT
today!!!
munch
crunch
KITTEN FOOD
munch
fooosh
KITTEN FOOD
munch
scritcha
KITTEN FOOD

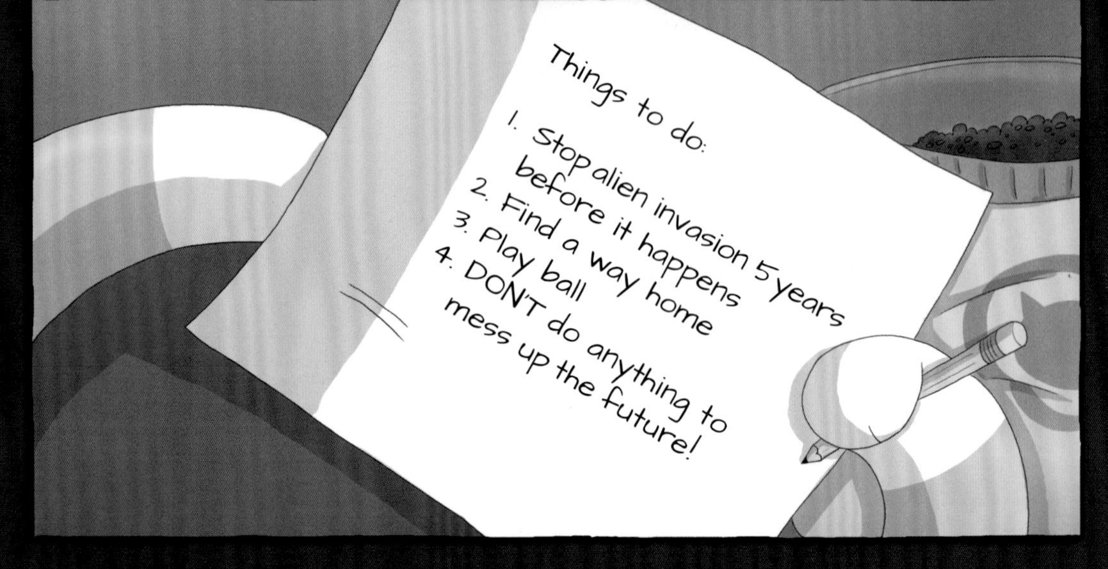
Things to do:
1. Stop alien invasion 5 years before it happens
2. Find a way home
3. Play ball
4. DON'T do anything to mess up the future!

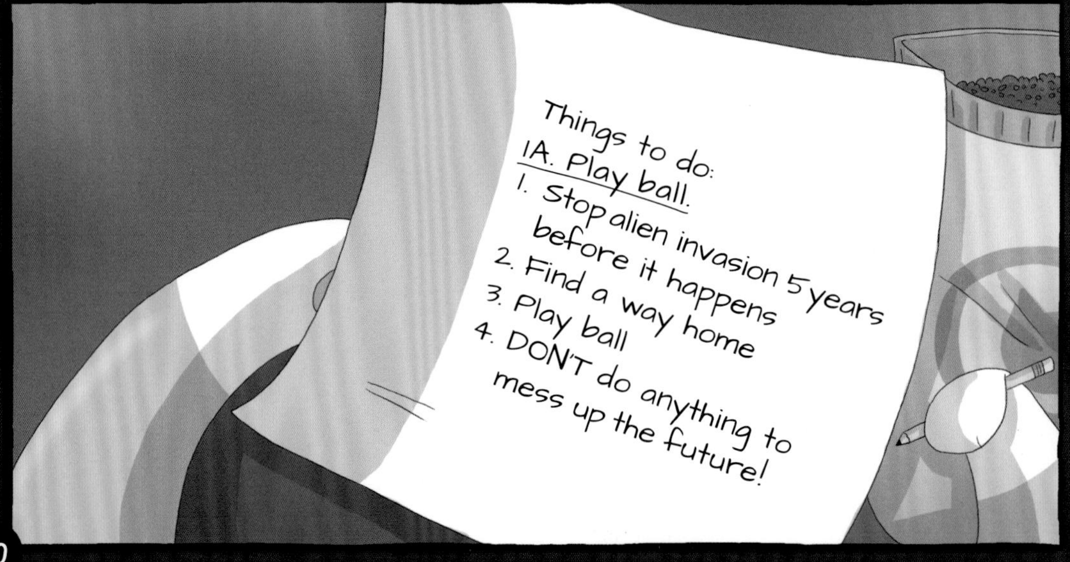
Things to do:
1A. Play ball.
1. Stop alien invasion 5 years before it happens
2. Find a way home
3. Play ball
4. DON'T do anything to mess up the future!

GORDON HAD BETTER GET GOING ON THIS LIST.
burp
NO TIME LIKE THE PRESENT!
OR IS THIS THE PAST?
urf
HE NEEDS TO CLEAR HIS MIND.

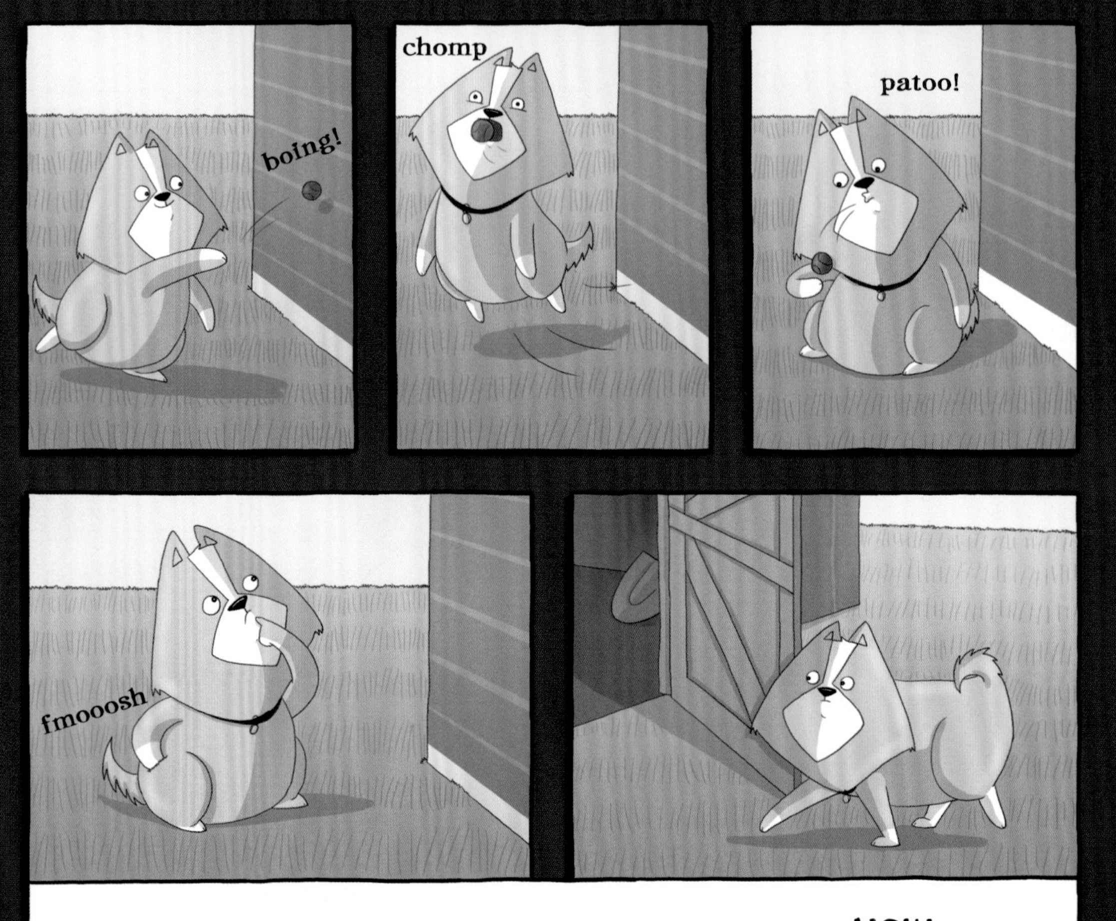
boing!
chomp
patoo!
fmooosh
THERE MUST BE A WAY TO PROTECT THE SPACE STATION NOW ...

SO THAT THE ALIENS CAN'T INVADE IN THE FUTURE.

scritch
ALL GOOD SPACE PETS KNOW THAT IF YOU WANT
TO KEEP YOUR SPACE STATION SAFE ...

weak point
weak point
THE FIRST THING YOU HAVE TO DO IS SECURE THE PERIMETER.

THE CRAWL SPACE SEEMS LIKE A GOOD PLACE TO START.

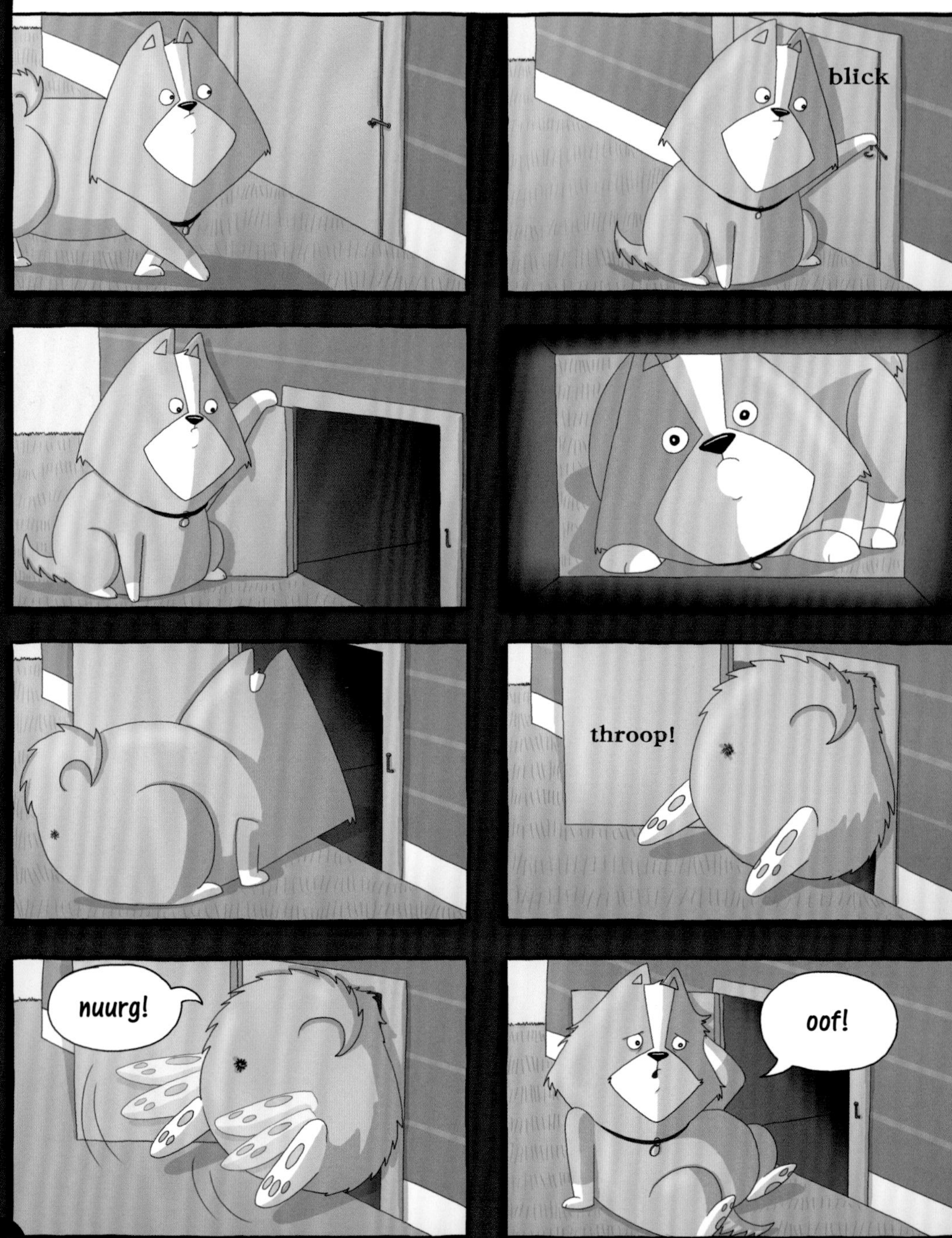

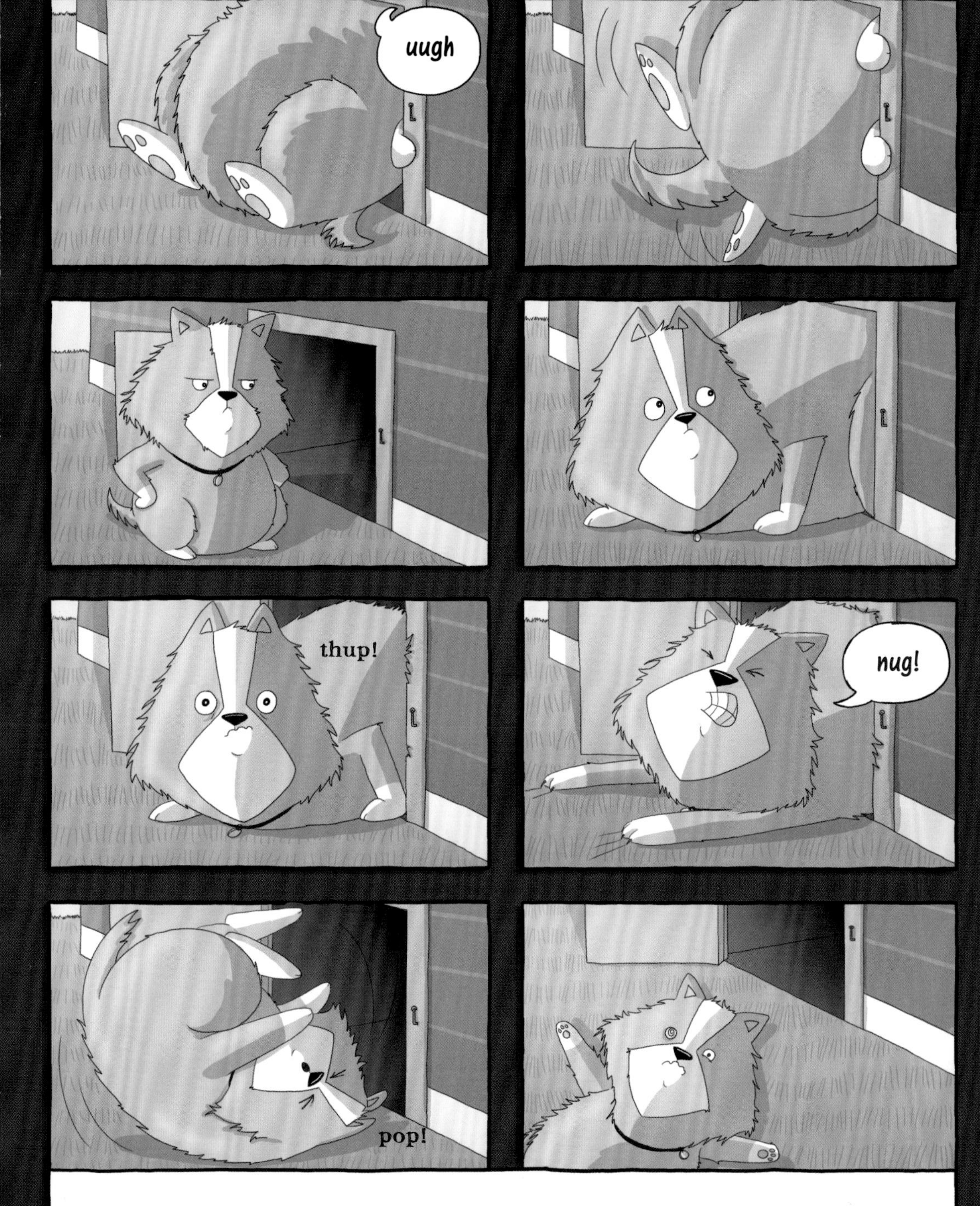

BINKY AND GRACIE ALWAYS MADE THIS LOOK SO EASY!

IF HE CAN'T GO UNDER THE SPACE STATION,
THEN MAYBE HE CAN GO OVER IT.

HE JUST HAS TO FIGURE OUT A WAY TO GET ON THE ROOF.

THAT'S IT ... HIGHER ...

JUST A LITTLE HIGHER ... **NOW!**

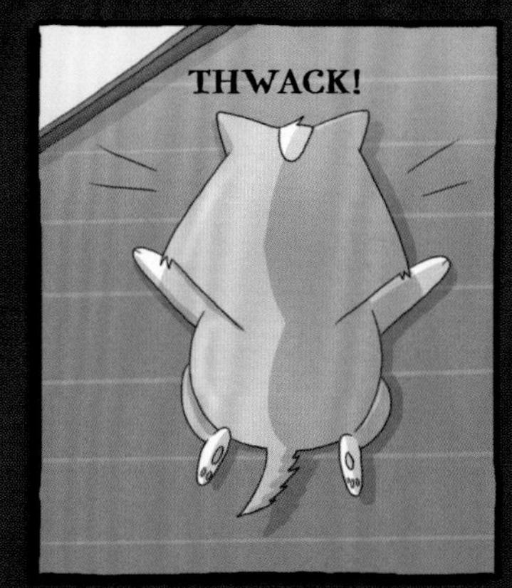

THIS ISN'T WORKING. GORDON IS AN INVENTOR, NOT A LEAPER.

IT'S TIME FOR HIM TO SOLVE THIS THE GORDON WAY ...

BY BUILDING AN ANTI-ALIEN ALARM SYSTEM!

HE DOESN'T HAVE MUCH TO WORK WITH ...

tinka
plook
BUT HE'LL MANAGE.

FINISHED! IT WILL LIGHT UP AND SOUND THE ALARM
AS SOON AS THIS PART SENSES ANY ALIEN ACTIVITY.

ZURP!

snurf

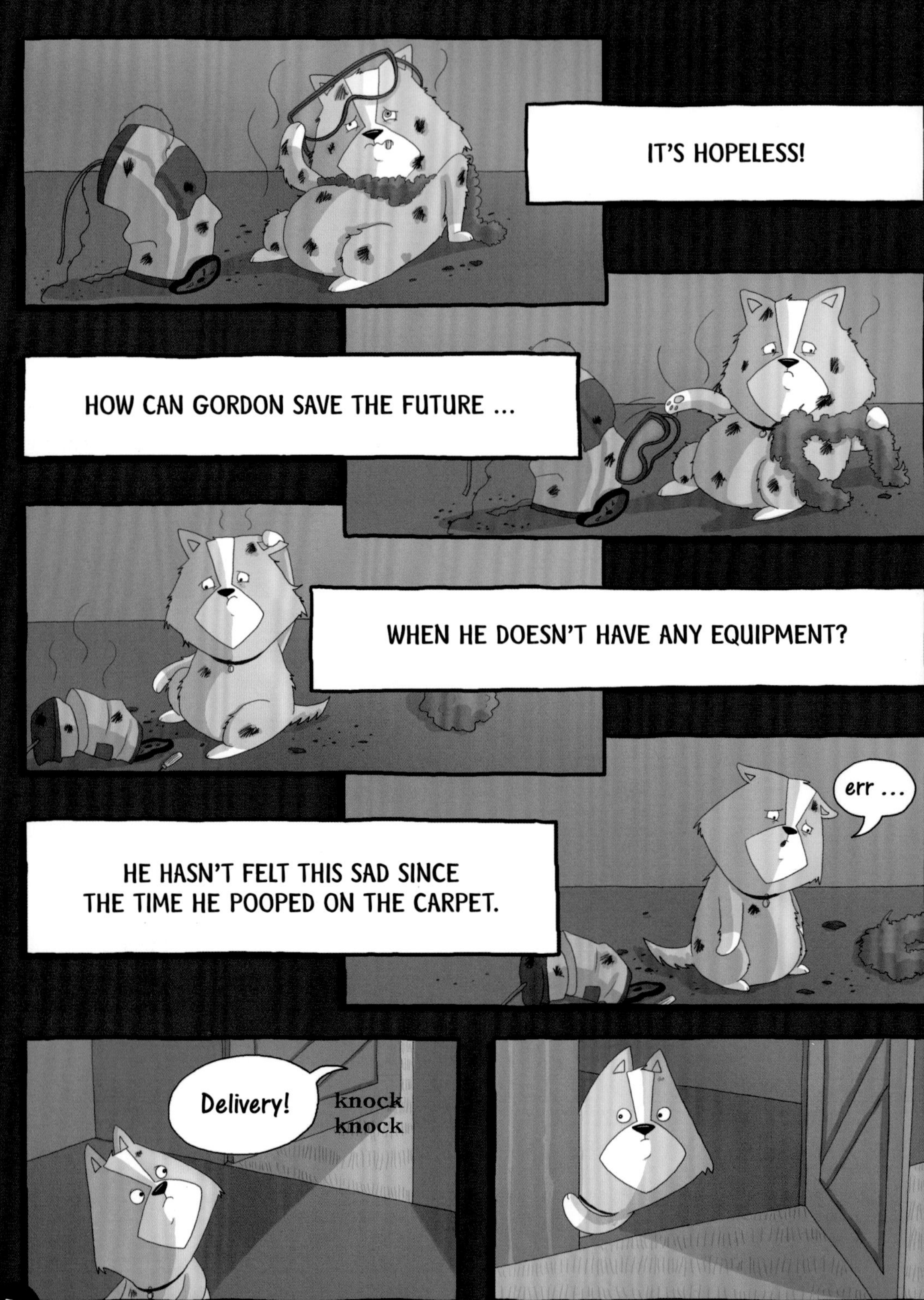
IT'S HOPELESS!
HOW CAN GORDON SAVE THE FUTURE ...
WHEN HE DOESN'T HAVE ANY EQUIPMENT?
HE HASN'T FELT THIS SAD SINCE THE TIME HE POOPED ON THE CARPET.
err ...
Delivery!
knock knock

Feline Agent Who
Is Not a Dog
292 Sentinal Pkwy
Dear Feline Agent Who Is Not a Dog,
I don't know who you are, but only a true F.U.R.S.T. agent would know how to find me when I'm deep undercover. For that reason, I've had headquarters send you ten millitails of allofuzzium. I hope our paths cross some day.
Good hunting,
Captain Gracie
HE KNEW HE COULD COUNT ON GRACIE.

THIS SHOULD BE JUST ENOUGH FUEL ...

FOR HIM TO STOP THE INVASION AND GET BACK TO THE PRESENT.

THE PRESENT MEANING THE FUTURE ...

GRRR! EITHER WAY, IT'S TIME TO SAVE THE DAY!

ALL RIGHT, BALL, LET'S GO HOME.

WAPOOSH!
DID IT WORK?
IS HE HOME?
BINKY!
slluuurrppp

wurf
woofa
snarfle
aroof
me-ow
GASP!
bzzzzz

RUN! IT'S A SWARM!
COME ON, BINKY!
urg

WHAT IS WRONG WITH YOU? YOU'RE A SPACE PET, NOT A ZOMBIE PET!
wave
snap

BINKY, STOP THEM! THEY ARE TOUCHING TED!
bzzzzzzzz

IT'S TED, BINKY!
NO ONE TOUCHES TED.
REMEMBER?!?

SOMETHING IS VERY WRONG.
WHAT COULD HAVE CHANGED BINKY ...
crunch
sniff
sniff
THIS MUCH?
LOW FAT
LOW CARB
LOW FLAVOR
GASP
hmmmmmmm ...

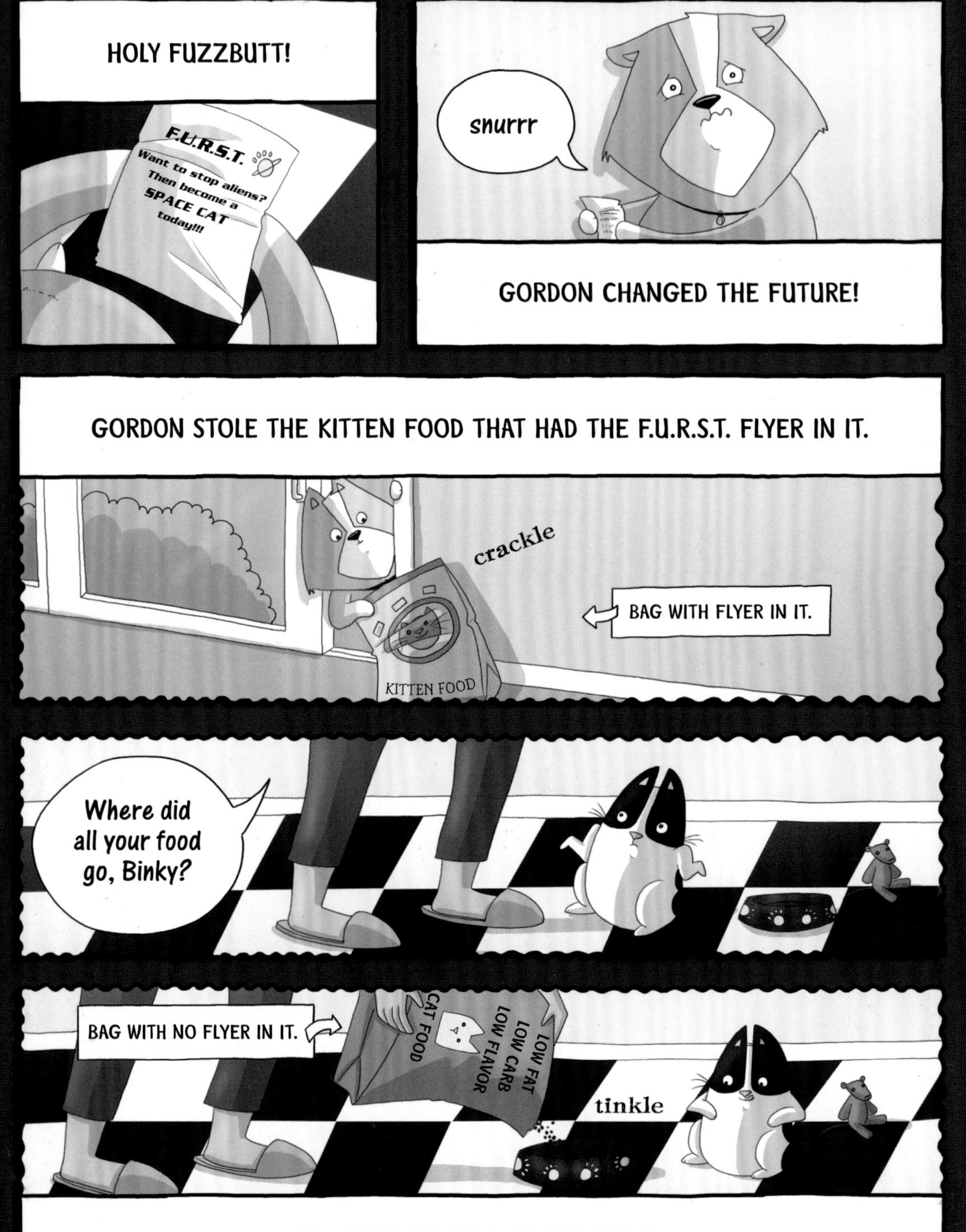
HOLY FUZZBUTT!
F.U.R.S.T.
Want to stop aliens? Then become a SPACE CAT today!!!
snurrr
GORDON CHANGED THE FUTURE!
GORDON STOLE THE KITTEN FOOD THAT HAD THE F.U.R.S.T. FLYER IN IT.
crackle
BAG WITH FLYER IN IT.
KITTEN FOOD
Where did all your food go, Binky?
BAG WITH NO FLYER IN IT.
CAT FOOD
LOW FAT
LOW CARB
LOW FLAVOR
tinkle
SO BINKY NEVER SAW THE FLYER.

AND SINCE HE NEVER SAW THE FLYER ...

HE NEVER BECAME A SPACE CAT!

THE ALIENS HAVE BRAINWASHED HIM TO NOT FIGHT BACK!

GORDON HAS TO FIX THIS.

BUT DOES HE HAVE ENOUGH ALLOFUZZIUM TO TRAVEL BACK FIVE YEARS THEN FORWARD AGAIN TO HIS TIME?

ALSO HE WILL HAVE TO TRAVEL TO THE MOMENT HE LEFT TO PREVENT A PARADOX, BECAUSE IF HE GETS STUCK IN THE PAST/FUTURE, THEN THERE WILL BE TWO GORDONS AND THE UNIVERSE WILL IMPLODE AND ...

IF HE LEAVES THE TIME MACHINE RUNNING ...

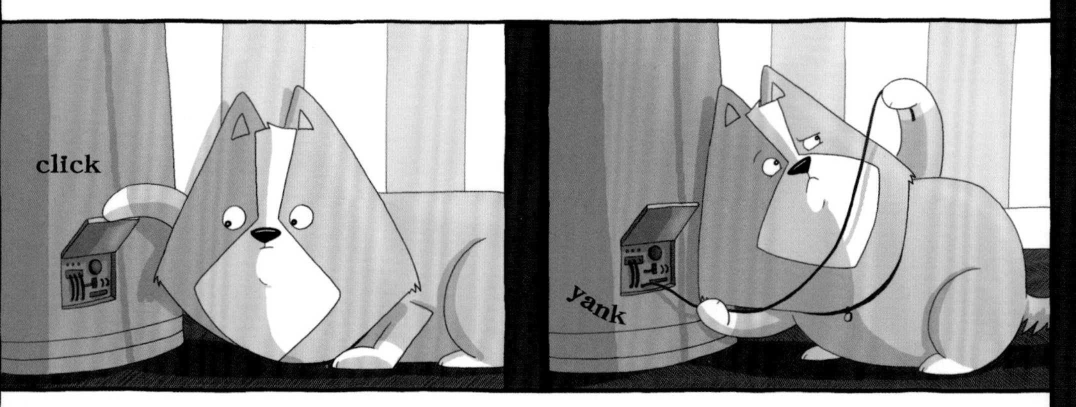

HE MIGHT SAVE ENOUGH POWER TO MAKE IT TRAVEL TWICE.

BUT HE WILL ONLY HAVE TWO MINUTES BEFORE IT AUTOMATICALLY TRAVELS BACK TO HIS TIME.

IF GORDON DOESN'T MAKE IT BACK TO THE TIME MACHINE BEFORE IT LEAVES, HE WILL BE STUCK IN THE PAST FOREVER.

BUT WHAT CHOICE DOES HE HAVE? HE HAS TO SAVE THE FUTURE!

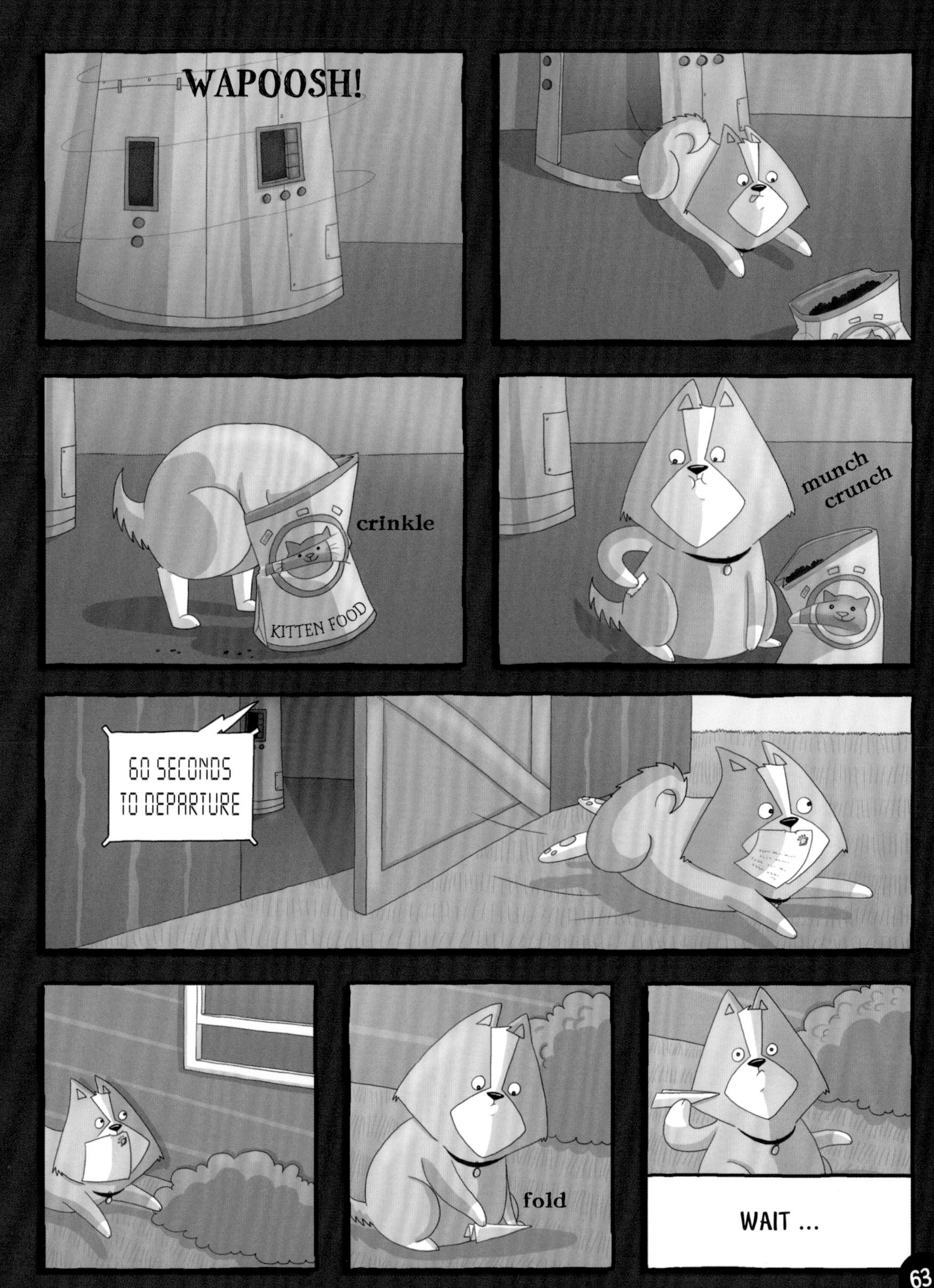
WAPOOSH!
crinkle
KITTEN FOOD
munch
crunch
60 SECONDS
TO DEPARTURE
fold
WAIT ...

EVEN IF HE FIXES THIS AND BINKY BECOMES A SPACE CAT AGAIN ...

THAT STILL DOESN'T SOLVE THE ALIEN INVASION!

HE'S ALMOST OUT OF TIME!
BUT THERE IS ONE LAST THING HE CAN TRY!

bzzz
5...
4...
3...

2...
huffa huff!
wrrrrrrr

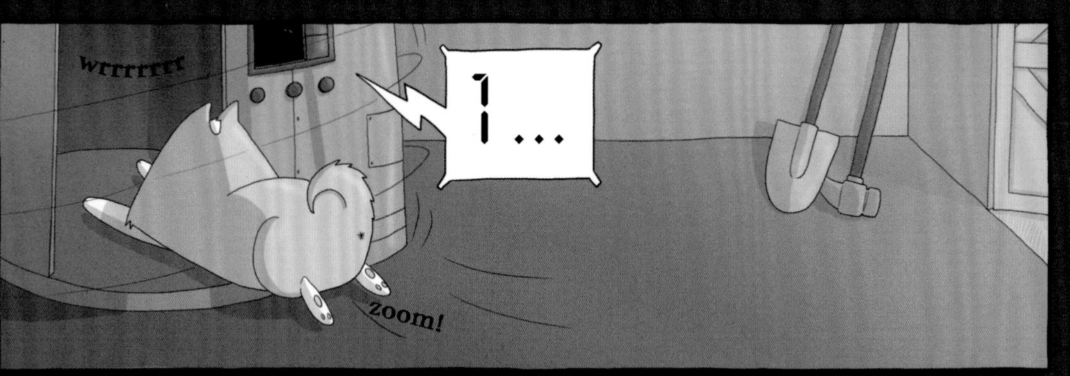
wrrrrrrr
1...
zoom!

SHAPOW!

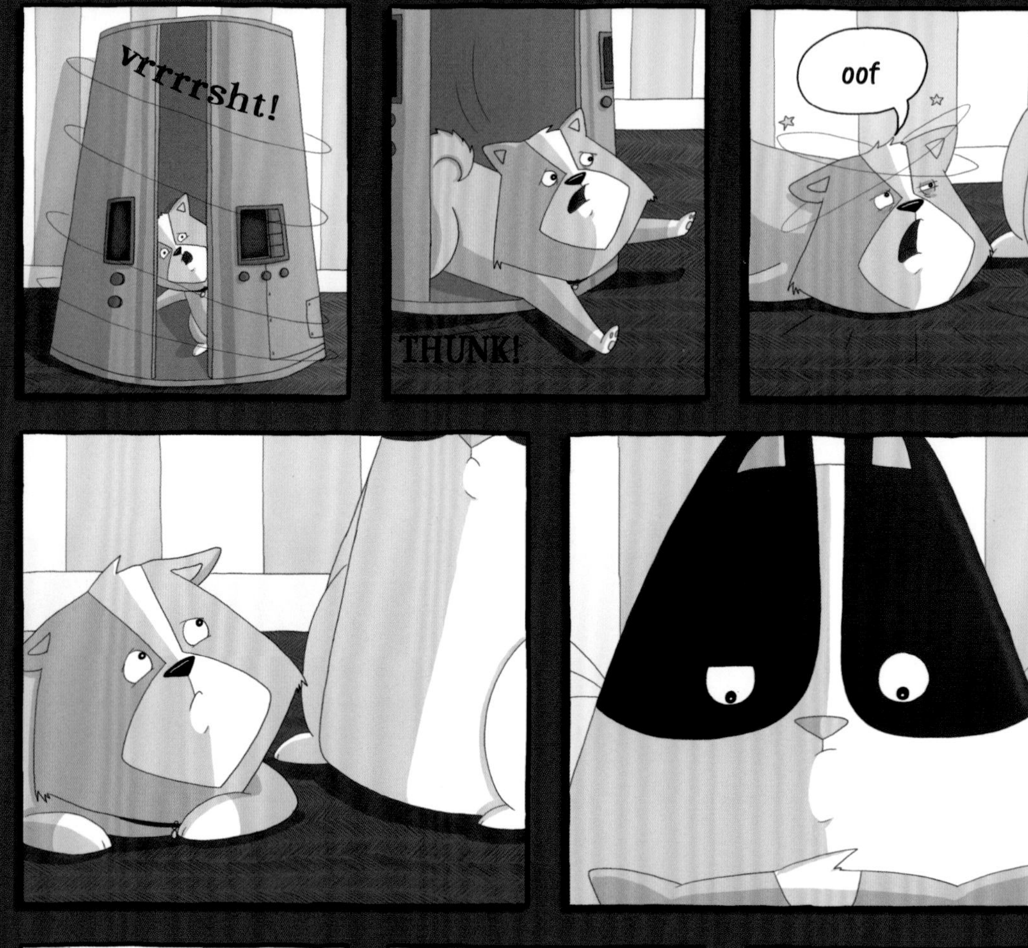
vrrrrsht!
THUNK!
oof

wave

smack

IT WORKED!

BINKY IS A SPACE CAT AGAIN!

GORDON IS HOME!

BUT WAIT.

GORDON STILL HAS TO STOP THE INVASION!

THERE WON'T BE AN INVASION.

BINKY HAD FIVE YEARS TO PREPARE.

THE ALIENS DIDN'T STAND A CHANCE ...

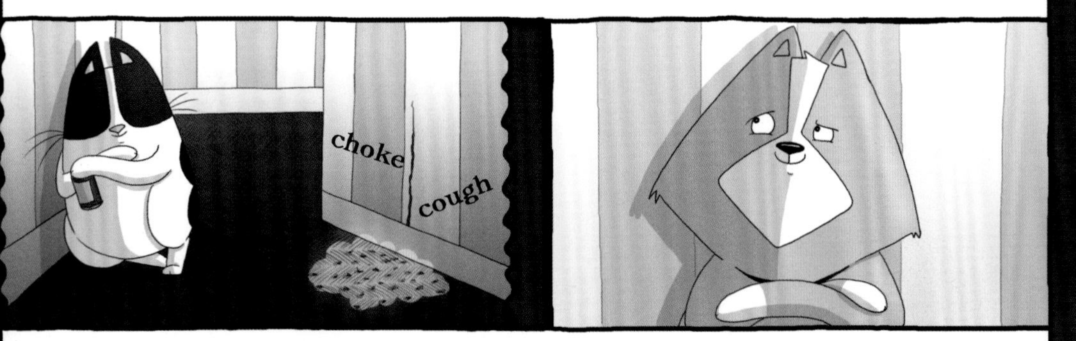

WITH GORDON TAKING CARE OF THINGS ... FROM THE PAST.

THANKS TO GORDON'S NOTE ...

HIS HUMANS, HIS FRIENDS AND HIS SPACE STATION ARE ALL SAFE.

THIS CALLS FOR A SNACK.

buzz?

bzzzzzz

SORRY, ALIEN.

TIME'S UP.

LOOKING FOR MORE LAUGHS?